PROUDLY HERS

Felicia Tyler

Felicia Tyler

Proudly Hers

Felicia Tyler © 2021

All rights reserved. This copy is intended for the original purchaser of this e-book only. No part of this e-book may be reproduced, scanned, or distributed in any printed or electronic form without prior written permission from Felicia Tyler.

This e-book is a work of fiction. While reference may be made to actual historical events or existing locations, the names, characters, places and incidents are products of the author's imagination, and any resemblance to actual persons, living or dead, business establishments, events, or locales is purely coincidental.

TABLE OF CONTENTS

PROUDLY HERS
CHAPTER 1
CHAPTER 2
CHAPTER 3
CHAPTER 4
CHAPTER 5
CHAPTER 6
CHAPTER 7
ABOUT THE AUTHOR

PROUDLY HERS
FELICIA TYLER

I don't think anyone gets married thinking they're going to get divorced down the road. I know I didn't. When my husband and I met in college, everything just seemed to fall into place. He was smart and could always make me laugh. He bought me flowers on Valentine's Day, gifts on my birthday, and didn't need a reason to surprise me or make me feel special.

Yet, somehow, something was missing.

I thought having children would fill that void. It seemed like the logical thing to do after we were married, and I held hope that being a wife and mother would fill the void in me that I'd felt all my life. We had two beautiful children, and I was blessed to spend many years at home with them as a homemaker and a mother.

By the time our children were grown and had moved away, things were different between my husband and me. He didn't surprise me anymore. He didn't buy me flowers. It seemed as though the spark between us had fizzled and died, and I wondered if it was him or I who had changed. I had accepted that, though we weren't the happiest, our marriage was convenient and familiar. I had settled into a life of comfort, and I thought I could be okay with it.

And then *she* happened, and I knew nothing could ever be the same again.

1

I could feel the warmth of the sun on my face, yet there was a sense of numbness welling up inside me that negated its beauty. I wanted to be happy. I wanted more than anything to be happy and grateful and content with my life and all that I'd accomplished.

But I wasn't.

The gnawing feeling of emptiness inside me had become overwhelming. Every day I woke up feeling drained and incomplete, no matter how many smiles I forced or conversations I had. No one could see my truth. No one could see the real me, buried behind the facade of a life I'd built, and I was left to suffer alone, in silence.

And then it happened. I met *her*.

It was a seemingly ordinary Saturday. I'd gone to the local market, as I did most Saturdays. For years I'd begged my husband to come with me, but he was always busy with work or sports or repairing something in the garage. Markets were my thing, he said, and insisted I'd have a better time on my own than with him there and miserable.

I was browsing through a cooler at one of my favorite shops, a quaint little place in the food sector that sold homemade pies. There were meat pies, fruit pies, and vegetable pies, all delicately seasoned and ready to be taken home and baked. I'd tried most of the flavors already but was excited when a spicy pear pie caught my eye. I went to grab one out of the cooler when our hands touched, and I felt a sensation, a soft tingling on my skin, that was foreign to me.

I immediately wanted to feel it again.

"Oh, I'm so sorry," the woman beside me cried, snatching her hand out of the cooler as she smiled at me. She looked to be around her mid-forties as well, with small crinkles in the corners of her bright green eyes, and a smile that took my breath away.

"Oh, that's okay," I said softly, silently admiring her beauty. She wore a lavender-colored dress that accentuated her feminine shape and an oversized sun hat. She didn't wear much makeup, but she didn't need it. She had a glow to her that I envied, with sunkissed skin that made it look as though she just got back from vacation. I wondered if she did.

"Do you come here often?" I asked, immediately regretting the cliched question.

Her smile broadened, and I felt a little less like a bumbling idiot. "I usually come on Sundays," she informed me, "But tomorrow I'll be out of town, so I came today instead. What about you? Do you usually come here on Saturdays?"

I nodded. "Yes, I always come on Saturday. I rarely miss one. That explains why I've never seen you here before. My name is Julie, by the way. Julie Conner."

"It's nice to meet you, Julie Conner. I'm Dana Walsh." She stuck her hand out, and my heart skipped a beat at the thought of her skin on mine once again. I nervously took her hand, my nerve endings drinking in the electricity between us. Her skin was soft and supple, yet my hand felt as though it were vibrating at her touch. I shook her hand, heartbroken when her skin parted from mine.

We paid for our pies and walked through the market together, chatting and enjoying one another's company. Something about Dana put me at ease as if she were an old friend I could tell anything to. We talked about the weather, our hobbies, what our children were like, what we did for a living, and the places we most wanted to visit in the world.

I learned that she had one grown son who'd moved abroad to teach English, that she lived alone with her two dogs and that she worked as a bank clerk. I told her about my two children and how I'd been married to the same man since college. She asked me what it was like being married, and whether or not I enjoyed it.

"I...Well, I'm a good wife," I told her. "My husband works hard. He's always worked hard to be a good provider and take care of our family, and I was fortunate enough to spend a lot of time with our children as they grew up. It's only been in the past four years that I realized I wanted to do more with my life, so I went back to school to become a librarian."

I wondered if she'd think that being a librarian was boring. A lot of people thought it sounded boring, but I was an avid reader and had always been happiest when surrounded by books. Still, not everyone saw the value in it, and some of my friends and family had wondered why I hadn't gone back to school for something better paying.

"That doesn't really answer the question of whether or not you're happy," Dana pointed out, and I could feel the heat rising off my face at her words. The truth was, I wasn't happy, but no one had taken the time to ask me that before. I never complained to anyone, and from the outside looking in, my husband and I had the perfect relationship. We were college sweethearts, owned a nice home, and had already started saving for retirement.

"I mean, every relationship has its ups and downs," I confessed, unsure of how else to answer. "Some days are definitely better than others."

"Well, the same could be said about life in general," Dana replied. "I think all that really matters is whether more of your days are good or bad, and how many of the good days are great." I looked at her and she smiled that warm smile again, and all I knew at that moment was that I didn't want to see her again.

I *needed* to.

"Dana, it's been lovely getting to know you," I told her. "Would you care to exchange numbers with me? I thought maybe we could get together for tea or coffee sometime. If you'd like to, that is."

"Give me your number," she instructed. "I'll send you a text and then you can save mine."

I went home that day filled with a gentle calmness that I hadn't felt in a long time. The pieces of me that were usually filled with anxiety had been quieted, and it felt like I could breathe for the first time in my life.

I didn't just go home with spiced pear pie. I went home with a feeling of hope.

2

Dana and I went for coffee the following Tuesday at a small downtown cafe near her condo. I hadn't been out anywhere besides work or the market in ages, and I hadn't realized how much I'd missed it. My senses felt alive with the unfamiliar sights and sounds, and my nostrils were flooded with smells of brewing coffee, freshly baked cinnamon buns, and Dana's subtle vanilla perfume. It was intoxicating, and I wished it would never end.

"This is my favorite place on Main Street!" she gushed, taking a deep breath in. "They always have great roasts, and all of their bread and desserts are baked fresh in-house. Seriously, everything is amazing. You should get one of the strudels! The cherry is great, but the blueberry is a close second."

Just seeing how happy the cafe made her warmed my heart, and I knew I'd have to bring her back here one day if I ever got the chance. We found a small table with two folding chairs near the front window. I watched happily as families and couples and smart-looking corporate people walked by, a tenderness growing in me at how sweet and content everyone looked.

I wondered if that would ever be me.

"So," Dana started, pulling me from my daydream, "Tell me more about yourself, Julie! I haven't had a new girlfriend to connect with in ages, and I'm excited to get to know you more."

I don't know if it was the fact that she'd said she wanted to get to know me or the fact that she'd referred to me as her girlfriend, but something made my breath catch in my throat. "There's honestly not much to know beyond what I told you at the market," I replied sheepishly. "Honestly, I live a pretty boring life."

She put her hands on mine, and I felt the same electricity between us as before. "There's not a single boring thing about you, Julie," she said, staring deep into my eyes. I felt as though I was being seen for the first time, and overwhelming feelings of elation and vulnerability came crashing over me, causing tears to form in the corners of my eyes.

"Thank you," I squeaked, fighting back my tears.

"There's nothing to thank me for," she assured me. "You deserve to know how interesting and unique and funny and brilliant you are. I know we don't know each other all that well yet, but I can tell you that getting to know you so far has been awesome. You should never feel like your life is boring. It can't be boring, because it's got you."

I should have stopped myself when I felt the impulse starting, but I couldn't. I leaned across the table and kissed her. It was soft at first, but the kiss slowly deepened. I kept waiting for her to pull away, to be repulsed by me and my actions and my impulsiveness.

But she didn't.

She leaned into the kiss, her hands tightening around mine. At that moment, I wasn't thinking about any of the onlookers that might be watching. I didn't think about the possibility of someone who knew me seeing me. There wasn't an ounce of fear in me. I was just lost in the sweet embrace of her lips, wondering why this felt so right while my brain was screaming that it should feel wrong.

By the time we broke off the kiss, the rest of the world had melted away, and nothing existed except her and me, sitting there in that cafe.

3

"I'm sorry," I told her, not knowing what else to say. Dana was still smiling at me, and I didn't honestly feel the least bit guilty or sorry for kissing her. Still, I hadn't asked or given her any sort of warning, and an apology for my boldness felt warranted.

"Don't apologize," Dana said. "If you're going to do something in life, anything, you should do it with conviction. Do it unapologetically. This way, you can take pride in your choices and know with confidence that everything you did was with purpose."

A server came over and asked if we'd decided what we wanted to order. She kept glancing at the table periodically, and it struck me as odd until I realized that Dana was still holding my hands. I thought I would feel embarrassed, or ashamed, sitting there holding hands with a woman whom I'd just kissed despite having a husband.

What I felt, however, was empowerment.

"I'm going to try the mac and cheese," I said confidently, "And I'll take a matcha latte with that. What about you, Dana?"

"I'll have the caesar salad and an Americano, please. Two creams, no sugar."

The server nodded, forcing an awkward smile to her face as she glanced at our hands again. "Sure, I'll have that out for you as soon as I can." She scurried off, and I couldn't help but feel as though she was in a hurry to get away from us.

"Julie," Dana started, once again pulling me from my thoughts, "Are you happy? You know, with your current situation and your life and everything? Because the way you kissed me made me feel like maybe you're not. Not that I'm complaining. I just think you deserve to be…you know, happy."

I hated that we were back to this question already. It meant that I had to face a harsh reality: I wasn't happy at all. I had to start answering tough questions, like why wasn't I happy, and what I needed to be happy, and why I had kissed Dana.

It wasn't like me to be so impulsive. What was it that being around her was doing to me? And why was it making me feel more alive than I'd ever felt before? Was I ready to face the truth and come clean about the fact that I might be…gay?

I'd never considered myself a lesbian. I'd gotten married at twenty, and had my first baby by twenty-two. Despite the fact that I was more attracted to my husband emotionally than sexually, I always thought we'd had a pretty good sex life. But kissing Dana was different, and I couldn't deny the fact that kissing her felt better than anything between my husband and I ever had.

Dana must have been able to tell from my face that my mind had become rampant with stress and questions. She squeezed my hands tighter again, and her smile once again began to effortlessly melt away my insecurities.

"Listen, we don't have to talk about all that today," she said. "We don't have to talk about all that ever if you don't want to. I'd be lying if I said I didn't hope to kiss you again someday, though." She had a sheepish grin on her face that only made her look more beautiful.

"Thanks, Dana. I'm sorry again for kissing you like that. I don't know what came over me."

"Seriously, Julie, you don't need to apologize," she assured me. "It was bold and spontaneous, and it's been a long time since I had any of that in my life. I was long overdue for something that breathtaking."

Our drinks came, and we wasted the afternoon talking and laughing and ordering strudels, enjoying the delicious food almost as much as one another's company.

4

Something was different in me when I went home that day and, despite my best efforts to hide it and act normal, my husband seemed suspicious the second I walked in the door. He eyed me up and down, his gaze narrowing.

"How was your time with…Who did you say you were with again, Dear?"

"Her name is Dana," I snapped. "I told you, I met her at the market last weekend, and our time together was lovely. We went to a cafe downtown and had lattes and some lunch. It was nice, she seems really cool." Even though it had been unfaithful to kiss Dana, I didn't appreciate the insinuation.

"Right. Which cafe did you go to?"

I paused, not unwise to how his eyes were challenging mine. If he thought he was going to catch me in a lie right now, he had another thing coming.

"It's called Buzzed. It's on the corner of Main Street and Twelfth Avenue. Look it up. I had the matcha latte and the mac and cheese, and both were very good. You should go some time."

My husband scoffed, seemingly disappointed at my quick answers. "You know I hate driving downtown, Jules."

"Well, that's too bad. You're really missing out," I shot back coldly. "Anyway, I'm tired and my ankle is really bothering me today. I'm gonna go lie down in bed and read my book for a while." I made my way to our room without either of us saying another word.

There wasn't much to say, really. I knew that my husband loved me, and overall he was a really good man, but we'd grown more and more distant over the past few years. It was no wonder he thought I'd made up a coffee date to orchestrate an affair, though he surely would have assumed it'd be with another man.

We hardly had sex anymore, and the romance in our relationship had been non-existent for half a decade at least. When we were younger, he'd been big into buying me flowers and gifts for Valentine's and my birthday, but that thoughtfulness had withered and died around the time we started having children.

A lot of days, I felt as though the children were the only thing really keeping us together, despite the fact they were both grown and out of the house now. I'd thought about the possibility of divorce before and how it would affect them, but I'd had no real reason to go through with it. My husband and I were cohabiting in the space just fine.

I wondered if that'd changed now.

As I crawled into bed with my crime novel, I couldn't stop thinking about Dana and the kiss. Her soft, sweet lips pressed against mine had been a light, parting the darkest clouds of my mind and helping me see what I'd been missing all those years. I'd been in denial for so long, disguising myself behind a curtain of marriage and children, that I'd actually started to believe it.

Now I was facing my truth, though, and I knew I couldn't stay content like this any longer.

5

Dana and I continued seeing each other over the next few months, shopping and flirting and trying all the different cafes in the city. Life felt so natural and easy when I was with her, and it didn't take long before I was addicted to her and the way she made me feel.

It wasn't until four months after our kiss that we ended up kissing again. This time she was the one who initiated it. We were standing under a large pendula tree in the park. My body burned with desire as she wrapped her arms around me and kissed me deeply, everything in me desperate to eternalize the moment.

When she pulled back, she stared lovingly into my eyes and told me that she'd fallen in love with me and didn't want to let me go. I tried not to cry as she said this, my heart welling with feelings of love and fear.

"I don't know what to do," I whispered, choking back tears. "I love you, Dana. I want to be with you, but...What will my children think? What will my husband think? What will my inlaws think? I've been with my husband for so long, I don't think anyone will accept this. What if I lose everyone in the process of becoming who I am?"

She thought quietly for a moment, her head cocked slightly to one side. "If you lost everyone, but gained yourself and your happiness in the process, would it be worth it?"

I placed my head on her chest and cried silent, happy tears. I knew she was right. I couldn't put off being myself any longer. As scared as I was, and as much as I didn't want to present everyone with my truth, it had to be done. I was suffering living this life. I didn't want to spend the second half of my life living the same lies.

As we sat there under that tree together, Dana helped me realize that the sooner I changed my situation, the sooner I'd be happy and free. She helped me come up with a plan, assuring me she'd be there to support me every step of the way, and offering to let me move into her place.

I knew I needed to tell my husband first, and I didn't want to waste another second. I drove straight home, my heart thumping out of my chest as my knuckles burned white on the steering wheel. Finally, after all these years, I was really doing this. I was finally going to be the out, proud gay woman I was meant to be, and I couldn't have felt more relieved.

When I got there, my husband's car wasn't in the driveway. It was odd because it was Saturday and he was usually watching sports or in his office focusing on his work, but I was too busy thinking about my own plan to give it much thought. I flew upstairs without stopping in any of the rooms, ready to pack my suitcase and get out of here.

It wasn't until later that I'd find the note sitting on the kitchen table.

6

Sadness is a funny thing. It has a way of creeping in, even in the happiest times. It took me about twenty minutes to pack my bag, making sure I'd gotten all my essentials. I knew I'd have to get a moving truck to move the rest of my stuff later, but I didn't want to waste another minute of my life being without Dana.

I went downstairs to make myself a cup of tea and wait for my husband to return home. Despite my plan to leave him, I still loved him and wanted to do the right thing by talking to him in person before I left. As I sat down at the kitchen table, patiently waiting for the kettle to boil, I saw the white piece of paper there, ominous and out of place.

My guts gnarled into a ball of emotion, my hands trembling as my eyes read each line. I scanned over it quickly at first, then reread it, giving each word several seconds to sink in. It turned out that my husband had been having an affair with a coworker, and the two had fallen in love and were relocating together.

By the time I read the note, my husband was already on a plane headed halfway across the world with another woman by his side.

I couldn't help but think that if he had left me for a man, it would have stung a lot less. Part of me was relieved, as this meant I didn't have to confront him about leaving him for Dana. Yet, another part of me felt betrayed, abandoned, and crushed. We'd been married for over twenty years. How could he just up and leave me for another woman?

Wasn't that what I'd been planning to do to him, though?

My heart and brain were at war with each other, fighting to determine which was more justified in its feelings. I sat at the table a long while, deflated and filled with a sense of emptiness. Then I did the only thing I knew would make me feel better.

I called her.

Dana came over without question or hesitation. She asked if I'd prefer to go back to her place, and I said I would. It was a short but quiet drive as I stared out the window and watched the city roll by against the setting sun.

When we got to her place, we sat on her couch and she wrapped her arms around me. She told me how everything happened for a reason, and how this was actually a blessing. She pointed out how my husband deserved a loving partner and happiness as much as I did, even if that partner was no longer going to be me.

I knew everything she was saying was true, but it was still a hard thought to comprehend. When I'd thought about leaving my husband for Dana, I hadn't thought about the idea of him being with anyone else. I knew it was only fair, but that didn't eliminate the pain.

I also didn't know how long he'd been having an affair, not that it mattered. I didn't truly want to know. But above all was the fact that he hadn't even given me the courtesy of a face-to-face goodbye. That hurt more than anything. I may have been planning to leave him for Dana, but I never would have left without a proper goodbye and explanation. After all we'd been through, I felt he deserved that, but him not feeling the same was a hard pill to swallow.

I sat there in Dana's embrace, hoping she would never let me go.

7

For a long while, I would go through bouts of sadness. Sometimes I would sit in my empty house and cry for hours. Other days, I couldn't have been happier to have Dana and to be finally living my truth.

Through all the ups and downs, Dana was planted firmly by my side. She was the sunshine my world had been missing. She always had a way of finding the silver lining in things, and it was her strength and positivity that comforted me and pulled me through my darkest days.

I was afraid to tell my children about everything that'd happened and all the changes, but my husband beat me to it. He didn't tell them about Dana and me, but he told them about his affair and how he'd moved away to be happy with the new love of his life. At first, the children were mad and turned against him, but it was Dana who managed to make them come around. She was the glue that kept our family together through the chaos, and the children grew to love her just as quickly and easily as I had.

As the months passed, the hurt subsided and everything started to feel normal again. My husband and I got divorced and sold our house. I moved into Dana's condo, and on our six-month anniversary, she proposed. Some people felt things between us were happening too quickly, but to us, everything was happening perfectly. I wanted to spend the rest of my life with Dana, and there wasn't a time too soon to announce it to the world.

That spring, Dana took me to my very first pride parade. I was overwhelmed with feelings of love and joy and acceptance. I met people in the community and made some new friends. I felt proud to be there, my fingers interlocked with Dana's as we watched all of the performers and floats go by. I'd waited over forty years for this, and life had never felt so worth living.

Although I was filled with pride to be a part of the parade, the proudest day of my life was the day I married Dana. We didn't want to waste any time and decided to tie the knot only six weeks after she proposed. It was everything I could have ever hoped for and then some. While my husband and I were young and had a modest wedding, Dana and I could afford our dream wedding, and she insisted we didn't spare any expense.

We decided to get married on a beach in Mexico. Dana owned a vacation property there, and it was where her parents' ashes had been spread. I think Dana could sense their spirits there that day, and she hoped they would have been proud of her if they could see how happy she was, and how in love we were with each other.

We said our vows with the beauty of the beach as our backdrop. Our bare feet pressed into the warm sand as we stared into each other's eyes, confessing our love for one another in front of all our friends and family. Our children cheered as the pastor pronounced us wife and wife, and we kissed more passionately than we ever had before.

I'd never felt more proud to be holding hands with another human being. Coming out had been a journey, but every step of the way was worth it because it led me to Dana's loving embrace. As much as I still cared about my ex-husband and wished him nothing but happiness and health, things between Dana and I were different.

She was the kindest, happiest, most loving person I'd ever met. She had an emotional strength and a sense of reason that I envied, and I knew there was no one alive who could possibly complete me the way she did. I'd waited half a lifetime to find her and, now that I had, I was never letting go.

"You know what the first thing I want to do when we get home is?" I asked her that night when we were back at her summer home.

"What's that?"

"Go to Buzzed and get a matcha latte and a strudel," I grinned.

Dana smiled. "Good idea," she said, leaning over and kissing me softly.

ABOUT THE AUTHOR

Felicia Tyler is your hottest new author of sweet lesbian romance! She's an advocate for equality, gay rights, living your truth, and love. Her stories are chock full of true love and happy endings and are sure to make any reader's heart swell.

THANKS FOR READING!

ABOUT THE AUTHOR

Felicia Tyler

Felicia Tyler is your hottest new author of sweet lesbian romance! She's an advocate for equality, gay rights, living your truth, and love. Her stories are chock full of true love and happy endings and are sure to make any reader's heart swell.